Great Minds

by PJ Gray

SADDLEBACK
EDUCATIONAL PUBLISHING
www.sdlback.com

All source images from Shutterstock.com

ISBN-13: 978-1-68021-152-8
ISBN-10: 1-68021-152-8
eBook: 978-1-63078-484-3

Printed in the U.S.A.

20 19 18 17 16   1 2 3 4 5

The bell rang.
It was time for lunch.

3

Tim sat by Lyn.
Li came over.
They were friends.
And they all played music.

"Hey," Tim said.
"I have an idea.
We can start a **band.**"

"Ooh!" Lyn said.
"I second that."

"Sure," Li said.

They met after school.
It was fun to play songs.
And to make new tunes.

"Hey," Li said. "We need a band name."

"Sure," Tim said. "How about LTL? Lyn. Tim. Li."

"Cute," Lyn said. "But no."

"Well," Tim said. "We are all smart. How about **Great Minds?**"

"Yes!" Lyn said.

"I like it," Li said.

Time went by.
They met most days.

"Guys," Lyn said. "We are good.
I say we put on a **show.**"

"Yes," Li said.

"Okay," Tim said. "When? Next week? Who will come?"

"Some friends," Li said.

"Yes," Lyn said. "But wait. **Not too many.** This is our first show."

PIZZA PIE

Pick Your Size
Pick Your Toppings
Save
10%
Order Now!

"Right," Tim said.
"What about food?"

"Pizza!" Lyn said.
"Keep it easy."

"I like that," Li said. "We can each buy one pizza."

"That is fair," Tim said.

"Yes," Lyn said.

A week went by.

It was the day of the show.

Nine friends came.

"Hi," Li said. "We hope you like the show."

The band played.
The song was a hit.

The band played four songs.
Then it was time for a **break.**

"Hey, guys," Tim said.
"I will call for pizza."

Great Minds

"Good," Lyn said.
"You each give me a ten.
I will pay when it gets here.
Will **three pizzas** still work?"

"Yes," Tim said. "Nine people
came. There are three of us.
That makes 12."

"That works," Li said.
"Four people for each pizza."

Tim made the call.

Li saw a friend.
She came up to Li.

"**WOW!** Your band is great!"

"Thanks," Li said. "I am happy you are here."

She held up her phone.
"I told some friends.
I want them to hear you too."

"Oh," Li said. "Cool. But there is not much room."

"No big deal," she said.

The break was over.
The band began to **play.**
Three girls came in.

The next song began.
Five guys came in.
Lyn saw them.
She shot Tim **a look.**
They played on.

The pizza got there.
It was time for a break.

Lyn paid. Then she shook her head. "We have a **problem.**"

"I know," Tim said. "What is going on? All these new people."

"**Sorry,**" Li said.
"My friend did that.
She thinks we are great.
She told her friends.
They came to hear us play."

Lyn was mad. "We have
more people than food.
What can we do?"

"Hey," Tim said. "They did not cut these pizzas."

Li took a look. "Weird."

"That helps us!" Lyn said.

"Yes," Tim said. "We can cut these. Just do the **math.**"

"Cut them like a pie," Li said.

"No, wait!" Lyn said.
"Cut them into **squares.**
And make more cuts."

pie cuts

square
cuts

"Yes!" Tim said. "More cuts. More pieces."

Tim cut the first pizza.
Four lines down.
Three lines across.

"I see 20 pieces," Li said. "We have three pizzas."

"That's **60** pieces," Tim said.

"Yes!" Lyn said.

A friend came over to help.
"You are so good!
What is your band's name?"

"Great Minds," Lyn said.

That made them all **grin**.

TEEN EMERGENT READER LIBRARIES

BOOSTERS

The Literacy Revolution Continues with New TERL Booster Titles!

Each Sold Individually

9781680211542

9781680211139

9781680211528

9781680211153

9781680211122